All Ladybird books are available at most bookshops,
supermarkets and newsagents, or can be ordered direct from:

Ladybird Postal Sales
PO Box 133 Paignton TQ3 2YP England
Telephone: (+44) 01803 554761
Fax: (+44) 01803 663394

A catalogue record for this book is available
from the British Library

Published by Ladybird Books Ltd
A subsidiary of the Penguin Group
A Pearson Company
© 1998 Cosgrove Hall Films

Based on The Animal Shelf created by Ivy Wallace

LADYBIRD and the device of a Ladybird are trademarks of
Ladybird Books Ltd Loughborough Leicestershire UK

The Animal Shelf

Music in the Woods

BASED ON THE ANIMAL SHELF CREATED
BY IVY WALLACE

Ladybird

One Saturday morning
Timothy's Special Animals were
playing some musical instruments.

"Hey, you lot, you're making a terrible noise," teased Timothy. "Would you like to help me to find some feathers in the wood?"

"Can we bring our instruments?" asked Gumpa.

"All right," laughed Timothy, and he loaded his Special Animals into his cart.

"I've an idea," said Timothy, when they reached the wood. "Let's split up, and if any of you gets lost, just play a few notes so we can find you."

"Brilliant!" said the Animals and went off to look for feathers.

Gumpa and Woeful looked closely over the forest floor. But soon Gumpa started to moan, "I haven't found a single feather yet. What about you, Woeful?"

But there was no answer. "Funny!" said Gumpa. "He was there just a second ago."

Just then Gumpa heard a harmonica playing, not far away.

Stripey and Getup heard it too.

"Woeful must be lost already," they cried. "Come on."

Woeful jumped out from behind a tree, as Stripey, Getup, Little Mut and Timothy arrived. "What's happening?" they asked.

"It's just Woeful being silly!" grumbled Gumpa.

"No, I wasn't," argued Woeful.

Timothy broke in. "Let's carry on hunting for feathers and, when you hear my drum, meet me at Splashing Stream," he said.

Soon the Animals were searching high and low. They each found a different feather…

a green one,

a brown one,

a black one,

a brown speckled one and

a red one.

Timothy was so pleased that he went straight home to look them up in a book. But the Animals decided to stay in the wood and make some music.

Gumpa wanted to be in charge.

"Quiet, everybody, I'm the conductor. Now follow me." Gumpa pointed to each animal in turn. But where was Little Mut?

At that moment, they heard a quiet whistle. "It's Little Mut! He must be lost!"

They searched in all directions for Little Mut. But instead they found a purple feather… and a parrot!

The parrot had been copying Little Mut's whistle. "We'll have to teach him another tune, so that we can find the real whistle," said Gumpa.

His plan worked and they traced Little Mut to a bush. He was stuck, and close to tears because he hadn't found a feather.

"Don't worry," said Gumpa, when he and Woeful had pulled their friend free. "You can give this purple feather to Timothy."

The parrot followed them down the path.

"Go home," Gumpa told him. "It's time to go home."

"Time to go home," repeated the parrot, but he stayed where he was.

"It's no good. He won't go," said Woeful.

"Won't go!" repeated the parrot.

So the Animals led him to Timothy, who took him back to his owner, Mr Trig, at the petshop.

The Animals followed Timothy and the parrot back to the petshop, and waited outside.

Before long Timothy came out and said, "Mr Trig was thrilled to have his parrot back. He gave me this bag of sweets… but of course, you deserve them really." Timothy shared them out.

As they turned to go, Gumpa couldn't resist one last tune on his trumpet. And its echo came back from the parrot in the petshop!